Here Comes Holi

Holi

The Festival Of Colors

Meenal Pandya

Published by:

MeeRa Publications
P.O.Box 812129
Wellesley, MA 02482-0014
USA

781 235 7441

www.meerapublications.com

Book Design and Cover by: www.mythicstudio.com

ISBN: 0-9635539-4-1

Printed in China

To

Shreedevi, Jayshree, and Yamal

For many colorful memories of Holi!

"Today is Holi!" Mom said.

"What is Holi?" I asked.

"It is a day to play with colors. Look outside and you will see," Mom said.

Outside, I saw a crowd of people having fun throwing colors at each other. Maya was filling her pichkari from a giant brass pot. Raju, Govind, and Abha were throwing colored powder at each other.

"Mom, why do people throw colors on Holi?"

"Let me tell you a story," Mom said.

Raju, Govind, and Abha also joined us on the porch.

We all settled on the swing.

"Once upon a time, thousands of years ago, there was a young prince named Prahlad. Prahlad was a very kind and happy prince. His smile made everyone happy. Everyone in the kingdom loved him and fulfilled his every wish. Prahlad was as happy as anyone could be.

But there was one problem.

His father, King Hirnakasyapu, was an Asura—a demon who was a cruel and unkind king. He thought of himself as the most powerful man on the earth. That is because, many years ago, he had done a very long penance for God Brahma to get special powers for himself. He prayed to God Brahma for days without eating or sleeping. When God Brahma appeared pleased by his penance, he asked God Brahma to grant him a wish that he could live forever.

After thinking for a little while, God Brahma said, "I cannot grant you that wish. But I can grant you a wish that:
You can never be killed by any man or animal,
You can never be killed by any weapon,
You can never be killed during daytime or night time,
and you can never be killed inside or outside any house or building."

Pleased with God Brahma's boon, the King came back to his kingdom, a very happy and proud man, for he was sure that now no one could ever kill him.

From then on, the strong and arrogant King demanded that everyone respect him more than anyone else, even more than any god, including God Vishnu, the god who looked after the entire Universe.

Everyone in his kingdom was afraid of him, and so they did as they were told.

But his own son Prahlad was different.

Prahlad had learned to respect God Vishnu from his mother and his teachers. He was not afraid of his father, even though he was only eight years old.

One day as he was playing on his father's lap, his father asked him, "Tell me my dear son, what have you learned in school? Who is the strongest in our kingdom?"

The young prince replied, "Father, I think it is you. You are the strongest in our kingdom."
The King, quite pleased with his son's answer, smiled and asked again, "Tell me my dear son, who is the strongest in the whole world?"

Prahlad thought for a moment and then replied, "Father, it is God Vishnu. He is the strongest in the whole world."

This answer made the King angry. He sent Prahlad away to school and told his teachers to teach him properly.

But again after a few months, when the King asked him the question again, Prahlad gave the same answer.

The answer made the King furious.

He ordered his army to bring a troop of wild and angry elephants. He asked the soldiers to tie the young prince and leave him on the ground. Then he sent these angry elephants to trample him. To the King's surprise, when the elephants came near Prahlad, a miracle happened. Instead of running over the little prince and killing him, the elephants bowed down to him and turned around.

Onlookers cheered in delight.

This made the King even more angry.

Then the King thought of a new plan.

The King had a sister named Holika who loved her brother very much and would do anything for him. Holika had a very special sari. This sari, although it looked like any other sari, was made of a special fabric that could never be burned by fire.

Knowing about this sari, the King asked Holika to help him. Holika agreed to do whatever her brother wanted.

He announced in his kingdom that the next day, when the sun went down, a special bonfire would be lit in the center of the town. In this fire, Holika would sit with the prince in her lap.

Everyone knew about Holika's special sari and the King's intentions of killing young Prahlad.

With sad faces and heavy hearts, they all gathered in the center of the town to bid farewell to their beloved prince. No one could eat anything that day, dreading what was to come.

At last, evening came.

In the center of the town, a huge fire was lit. Holika was ready with her special sari wrapped around her and took Prahlad in her lap. Not knowing his aunt's evil intentions, he felt safe in her lap. But everyone else was worried.

As the orange flames touched the sky, people's hearts sank in deep sorrow.

They all expected that Holika would come out of the fire unharmed and their beloved prince would be burned to ashes.

But what they saw was different. It was Prahlad, their beloved prince, walking out of the fire—unharmed and smiling instead of Holika.

Prahlad said that a strong gust of wind came and the sari came undone on Holika and covered him protecting him from the fire. Prahlad told everyone that he had promised his Aunt Holika, when she asked for forgiveness, that in her memory this day would be called Holi, and everyone would celebrate Holi with colors to re-member her.

That is why, even after thousands of years, on the day of Holi, peo-ple throw colors at each other and rejoice," said Mom as she fin-ished her story.

We played with the colored water, abil, and gulal all day with all our friends, uncles, aunts, and grandparents.

In the evening, I took a bath. I loved the new clothes Mom had for me. After taking the bath, we all went to the center of the town where a huge bonfire had been lit.

We sat around the fire praying and thinking about brave Prahlad and his Aunt Holika.

When we came home, Mom had prepared my favorite dinner.

Mom was right. Holi is fun. At bedtime, I remembered how much fun I had all day. Just then I remembered Prahlad and his story.

"Mom, what happened to Prahlad and the King after Prahlad came out of the fire?" I asked.

Mom smiled and continued her story.

"When the King saw that Prahlad came out of the fire alive chanting God Vishnu's name and that his beloved sister had burned to ashes in the fire, he became very angry. He asked, "Where is your God Vishnu?"

Prahlad replied, "He is everywhere."

So the King asked, "Is he in this palace? Is he in this room? Is he in this iron pillar?"

Prahlad said, "Yes, of course."

The King ordered his servants to heat up the big iron pillar. He asked them to make it so hot that it would glow all red. Then he told Prahlad, "If you think God Vishnu is in this pillar, then go and hug the pillar, or agree that I am stronger than your God Vishnu."

Prahlad thought for a moment.

Looking at the red-hot iron pillar, he was frightened. But as he squinted his eyes at the pillar, he saw a long line of black ants crawling upwards! "If those ants can climb the pillar, it cannot be that hot, so why should I be afraid?" he thought.

So, to everyone's amazement, he ran and hugged the big, fat, red-hot pillar with his two tiny hands while chanting the name of God Vishnu.

Everyone in the King's court gasped.

But wait! Why is the pillar cracking?

With a thunderous sound the pillar cracked open and out came a strange-looking creature that was half-man and half-lion.

"I am Narsimha," said the creature, "and I am here to protect you all from the evil King."

For the first time in his life, the King felt a strange sense of fear at the sight of Narsimha. He ran for the door, but Narsimha grabbed him and dragged him on to the doorstep of the castle.

The frightened King remembered God Brahma's boon and told Narsimha, "you cannot kill me inside or outside of any house or castle."

"You are right," Narsimha said, "But we are on the doorstep—neither inside nor outside."

The King said, "God Brahma gave me his boon that no man or animal can kill me."

"Yes, but I am neither man nor animal. I am Narsimha, half-lion and half-man," came the reply.

Then Narsimha reminded the King that it was then evening time, neither daytime nor night time.

Now the King was really frightened.

"But…." he stuttered, "I cannot be killed by any weapon."

"True," said Narsimha, "I do not need any weapon. My claws are strong enough."

Saying that, Narsimha killed the evil King. Everyone in the entire kingdom rejoiced. They declared Prahlad to be their new King and lived happily ever after."

Mom smiled as she finished the story and tucked me into bed.

ABOUT HOLI

Holi is a spring festival and has been celebrated for thousands of years in India and by Hindus around the world. It is one of the most joyous festivals because it crosses all boundaries of age, religion, caste, and gender.

In many parts of India, on the day of Holi, people observe fasting by only eating popcorn and puffed rice. Then in the evening, after the bonfire is lit and everyone has prayed around it, they come home and eat a special dinner.

In some parts of India the bonfire is lit on the eve of Holi.

Holi is also associated with Lord Krishna and his beloved friend Radha. There are thousands of folk songs and poems written on Krishna and Radha playing Holi.

A special dance called Dandia Raas, which is played with a pair of sticks, is considered to be the dance of Krishna and Radha.

Lord Krishna is said to have killed a demon named Putna on the day of Holi.

The day after Holi is called Dhuleti and is also celebrated by many, especially in the northern part of India.

GLOSSARY

- abil: White powder used as part of religious ceremonies as well as during Holi celebrations
- asura: A demon
- Brahma: The God of Creation, part of a trinity in Hindu mythology
- dandia raas: A dance played with small wooden sticks called dandia
- gulal: Red colored powder used as part of religious ceremonies as well as during Holi celebrations
- Krishna: One of the incarnations of God Vishnu
- Narsimha: One of the incarnations of God Vishnu in the form of half lion and half man
- pichkari: Water gun used to spray colors on the day of Holi
- Radha: Krishna's beloved friend and a consort
- sari: Long fabric wrapped around as a dress worn by women in India
- Vishnu: The God of the Universe, part of a trinity in Hindu mythology